Dragon Hunter

Contents

Claire Llewellyn
Character Illustrations by Jon Stuart

Steck Vaughn

HOUGHTON MIFFLIN HARCOURT
Supplemental Publishers

www.SteckVaughn.com
800-531-5015

Dragon Stories

About 100 years ago, people began to hear stories about real-life dragons. The stories said that the dragons lived on a tiny island called *Komodo*.

Look out! It's a dragon!

An **explorer** in New York heard about the dragons. He wanted to go to Komodo. He wanted to find out if the stories were true. The explorer's name was *W. Douglas Burden*.

EUROPE

NORTH AMERICA

ASIA

New York

AFRICA

SOUTH AMERICA

KOMODO

AUSTRALIA

Komodo is a long way from New York.

The Island of Komodo

Burden sailed to Komodo. He took a team of people with him. He wanted to catch a dragon and take it back to New York. He thought that the rest of the world would like to see a real dragon.

Burden had to share his camp with spiders and snakes!

Green Tree Viper

Golden Silk Spider

When Burden and his team got to the island, they made a camp. Then they went to look for the dragons. They found many amazing animals, but no dragons.

Discovering the Dragon

For many days, Burden explored the island. Then one day, he saw a huge new footprint in the mud. Then he heard a noise. He looked up and saw a giant beast.

claws

Its head moved from side to side. It had sharp teeth and claws. It had a long forked tongue. Burden had **discovered** a dragon!

eye

head

Help! A dragon!

tongue

A Dragon Trap

Burden called the beast a *Komodo dragon*. He wanted to catch one to take back to New York. So he and his team made a trap. They put some food inside it. Then they waited.

Do you think it's right to trap a wild animal?

Finally, a huge Komodo dragon came to eat the food. The dragon got stuck in the trap. Burden locked it in a cage, but the dragon was very strong. The next day, it was gone. He never saw that huge dragon again.

Dragons on Display

In the end, Burden trapped two smaller dragons. He took them back to New York and gave them to a zoo. He also gave some stuffed dragons to a **museum**. The museum put the dragons on display. You can still see them in New York today.

Burden's dragons on display in the *Museum of Natural History*, New York

Komodo dragons are very special. They only live on one tiny island. They are not used to living anywhere else. So people have to take very good care of the dragons in the zoo. Otherwise they will get sick.

a Komodo dragon in a zoo

Komodo Dragons

Komodo dragons are giant **lizards**. They use their tongues to taste the air. This helps them to find food. They can find an animal from 2 miles away!

Komodo dragons are dangerous. Their mouths are full of deadly **germs**. If they bite an animal, the germs will kill it. The dragons sometimes bite people, too. You have to be very careful around Komodo dragons!

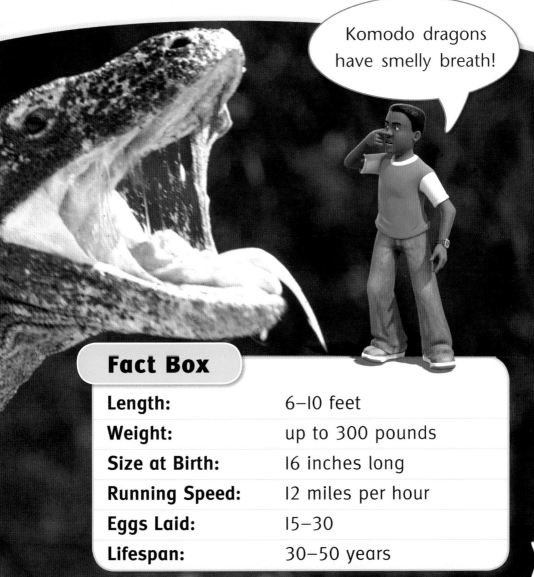

Komodo dragons have smelly breath!

Fact Box

Length:	6–10 feet
Weight:	up to 300 pounds
Size at Birth:	16 inches long
Running Speed:	12 miles per hour
Eggs Laid:	15–30
Lifespan:	30–50 years

New Discoveries

Komodo dragons still live on Komodo. There are about 5,000 dragons alive today.

Are there any other animals still to be discovered? Yes! All these animals have been discovered in the last few years. Who knows what other amazing animals are out there?

Discovered

a Purple Sea Star—discovered in the United States

Discovered

a Yariguies Brush-finch—discovered in South America

Discovered

a Highland Mangabey—discovered in Africa

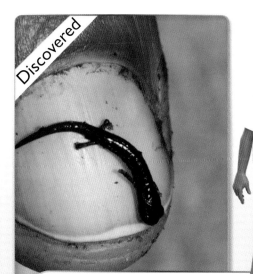

Discovered

a Dwarf Salamander—discovered in South America

If you were an explorer, what kind of animal would you like to find?

Glossary

discover   to find out about something

explorer   a person who travels to places that we do not know much about

germ   a tiny, living thing, too small to see; some germs can make you sick

lizard   an animal with scaly skin

museum   a place where interesting things are kept for people to go and see

Index